RICH MAN, DEAD MAN

Another in

The Tanner & Thibodaux Series

Larry Watts

Lone Writer Publishing

RICH MAN, DEAD MAN
A Tanner & Thibodaux Crime Novel

Inquiries to
Lone Writer Publishing
2874 Morning Pond Lane
Dickinson, TX 77539

ISBN – 978-0-9890859-6-0

Library of Congress Control Number: 2014911214

This is a work of fiction. All characters and events depicted herein are fictional and the product of the author's imagination.

Published in the United States

As with all my writing, special thanks to my wife, Carolyn Ferrell Watts, a fellow author and inspirational partner.

Thanks also to my author friends Rene' Palmer Armstrong, Gloria Hander Lyons, and Tom Rizzo for their editing, titling and cover design advice.

Chapter 1

"You'll never leave here, son. The only question for you is, how much do you want to suffer before you go to the other side?" The words were cold, calm, and almost sexual, coming from the well-dressed man in his late forties. He had become all too familiar to Devin Blakemore in the last 12 hours.

A feeling that everything seemed unreal dulled Devin's senses. At the moment he'd spotted the man climbing from a black Mercedes it occurred to him that such a person didn't belong in a place like this musty smelling, dimly lit warehouse. The man's clothes were immaculate and he was cautious to avoid the one dusty table in Devin's view. Manicured fingers adjusted a golden cufflink clasping the end of his tailored sleeve. Elliott reeked of wealth.

He watched now as the man nodded to Omar once again. Smiling, Omar reached for the pliers that lay on the small table next to the chair where Devin's friend, Trey Ward, slumped forward as far as the rope around his chest allowed. Devin shuddered at what he knew was coming next for his friend.

Omar used the pliers to clamp the joint of Trey's right thumb, pulling his arm to the side so that the hand was resting on the table with thumb extended. He then picked up a bloody meat cleaver and chopped the thumb from Trey's hand. Trey screamed, not as loud as he had when the pinky and index fingers had been taken, but still a sickening sound.

Devin's left eye was swollen shut, the right nearly so. Both were bloody from the beating Omar administered just after the two friends were tied to the chairs. But if he turned his head slightly and tilted it back, he could still see Trey, who suffered the worst of Omar's torture once he tired of using his fists to beat Devin first and then Trey.

Elliott told the two friends he wanted a simple question answered, after which he had assured them in a very calm, matter-of-fact voice, that they would be put to death quickly and with as little pain as possible. *Where was the money the two owed him for the most recent shipment of heroin they were supposed to have sold for Omar?*

It was the second time in as many months the two failed to deliver the profits to Omar. The first time, Trey wasted half the money betting on professional football games. Omar gave them two weeks to come up with the money. But they misread his reprieve as generosity. Then, the night before they were to meet Omar with the money from a second shipment as well as the missing money, they were robbed by another street dealer.

Omar was not happy. He didn't need to physically overpower them because he was an imposing figure. Neither of the young men considered challenging him. Within minutes both were handcuffed, loaded into the back of a van and driven to where they now sat, tied to chairs in the middle of the warehouse. The question posed by Omar was simple. But neither knew the answer. They didn't know who robbed them.

"Stop," Devin blurted. "I'll tell you where the money is. Mikey Jackson and two of his buddies robbed us before we could get the money to Omar."

He slumped in the chair, aware he and Trey had little time left. Mikey was probably doomed as well, but the torture was more than he could tolerate.

Omar walked to the van parked inside the warehouse. Elliott moved toward the black Mercedes parked behind the van, opened the driver's door and sat down. A second later the engine revved, the overhead door of the warehouse opened, and Elliott drove away. Devin heard crickets chirping in the night. By twisting his head, he could see well enough to tell there were no lights outside. They must be far out of the city.

Omar turned from the van with an automatic pistol in one hand. He walked to Trey. Blood formed puddles beneath him as the stumps of his severed fingers continued to bleed. Omar pulled his head back by the hair. When he released it, Trey's head bounced forward as if his neck was broken. He lost consciousness from loss of blood combined with the terror of the night.

The drug dealer turned to Devin. "You'll have to load him in the van." He untied the rope and removed the handcuffs from Devin's wrists.

Devin stumbled to his feet as Omar returned to Trey's chair. He raised the pistol and fired one shot into the back of Trey's head. The ravaged body barely registered shock as the bullet entered, but Devin jumped and cringed. As the two men dragged Trey's body toward the van, Omar's foot became tangled in the rope that had been removed from Trey's chair. Before he could regain his balance, he fell to the floor. The pistol dislodged from his waistband, hitting the floor and sliding out of reach.

Devin seized the opportunity. He raced out the door into the dark night. Eyes swollen and nearly blind from the beating; the darkness made little difference to his sight. He tripped and staggered, but he didn't stop running, on and on into the night.

Chapter 2

Calvin Thibodaux sat on his couch watching the local San Antonio news. The body of Trenton Ward's only son had been discovered earlier in the day along a country road south of San Antonio. The reporter on the scene stared into the camera as she reported that sources close to the investigation had revealed that Trey Ward appeared to have been tortured and his body mutilated before his death.

The identity of the victim as Trenton Ward's son was enough to make this a story that would play out for years to come. Trenton was San Antonio's wealthiest and most influential citizen. His investments included real estate, banking, ranching, and professional sports teams. The tentacles of his business reached across the nation and to every foreign shore with an opportunity for American enterprise.

Thibodaux's interest in the story was no greater than that of other residents of Success, Texas, a small community situated about an hour by car from the larger city of San Antonio. He and his friend, Milo Tanner, worked together on a few private investigations, but there was little chance a big city murder would end up on their agenda. Most of their work involved employee theft and missing persons.

When Thibodaux retired from the military, he planned to return home to Success, start a small landscaping business, and live a quiet life. The murder of his niece changed his relatively passive lifestyle. He asked Tanner, a retired Houston cop, to look into the case. And he had assisted his new friend in that task.

Thibodaux joined the Army at twenty, intent upon becoming a Ranger and was accepted into the 75th Ranger Regiment. At that point, the U.S. Army Delta Force recruited him. He received more training and tougher assignments than he ever anticipated.

The incursion of Iraq into Kuwait, which triggered the U.S. response named Desert Storm and events surrounding the World Trade Center tragedy, made him a long-term resident of the Middle East. Eventually his unit spent much time in Afghanistan and Pakistan developing intelligence and conducting covert operations in the effort to hunt down Osama Bin Laden. Thibodaux learned how to kill silently, smile broadly, and put yesterday out of his mind.

Despite all the training, he couldn't overcome his need to seek revenge when his niece was murdered. He and Tanner became such fast friends during the case, they decided to team up and offer private investigative services. Neither needed the income, but both enjoyed working together and maintaining their professional skills.

Thibodaux still kept a few landscaping customers simply because he liked the serenity of mowing lawns, shaping hedges, and planting flowers. It was therapeutic to the man who had experienced so much.

*****

Three months after the discovery of Trey Ward's body, Thibodaux and Tanner sat at the Dry Gulch Saloon in Success, nursing beers. The Dry Gulch was a gathering place for many of Success's residents. Socio-economic and racial differences didn't exist in the old house that had been converted years ago into a bar. If you sat in a corner, people respected your privacy. If you wanted conversation, it was readily available as well.

"Randy called me yesterday and asked me to drop by," said Tanner. "I saw him this morning. He wants me to meet with Trenton Ward about the death of Ward's son. Want to ride to San Antonio tomorrow?"

"What did the Sheriff say Ward wanted?" Thibodaux knew that Tanner always called the sheriff Randy, but never became comfortable with the informality, even though he knew the sheriff wouldn't have minded.

"Didn't say. Just told me that he's known Ward ever since they attended Texas A&M at the same time and reconnected after Randy became a San Antonio cop. He said Ward asked him for a name of someone who might look into his son's murder." Tanner drained the last of his beer.

"I guess I'm missing something," Thibodaux responded. "I thought that guy, what was his name, Omar something or another, pled guilty to murdering the Ward kid in return for a life sentence instead of chancing the death penalty."

"Omar Stallings. He did plead on the murder. I have no idea what Ward wants.

"I'll pick you up at about eight in the morning."

*****

The drive to San Antonio was uneventful. Tanner pulled into a parking space at the building located not far from the airport, on the north side of downtown. They rode the elevator to the fourteenth floor. The offices of Trenton Ward reflected exclusivity and wealth. The cost of the marble and stainless steel in the reception area alone was as much as a working man's mortgage.

When Tanner told the young, attractive receptionist about his appointment, she appeared skeptical and almost hesitant to call Trenton Ward. Neither man wore a jacket nor a tie. Nearly all those who came to see her boss dressed in business attire. In seconds, however, upon hearing their names, her expression changed.

"Mr. Ward is waiting for you. Right through those doors," she said as she pointed to a gigantic set of double doors on her left.

Upon leaving the foyer, a second young woman, even more attractive, ushered them along a hallway and into a large, expensively-appointed office. A meticulously groomed, tall, trim man expensively outfitted in a tan suit and tie stood to greet them in front of his desk.

"Mr. Tanner. Thank you for coming," he said as the two shook hands. "I'm Trenton Ward."

Turning slightly toward Thibodaux, he extended his hand again.

"Trenton Ward," he said. His quizzical facial expression was an unasked question.

"I'm Thibodaux."

"Please, both of you; have a seat," Ward gestured toward a small conference table to the right of his desk.

After all three sat down, Tanner picked up the conversation again. "Thibodaux is my partner. How can we help you, Mr. Ward?"

Ward glanced back at Thibodaux, clearly not expecting a third person in the conversation.

"I would like to speak candidly, Mr. Tanner. I was not anticipating that you would have a companion."

"We work together," replied Tanner, in a slightly irritated tone. "If you can't say it with Thibodaux here, you probably shouldn't say it at all."

"I understand, Mr. Tanner. You come highly recommended by Sheriff Jackson. I didn't mean to imply anything at all. Let me have my assistant bring in some coffee and pastries." He touched a button on the corner of the table and gave instructions to his secretary.

Chapter 3

Ward began by recounting the story of the death of his son. He added details neither of his guests heard before.

"It's never been released by the media, but there was another young man with my son the night he was murdered. Devin Blakemore was a friend and apparently a partner in selling dope with my son. He escaped before he met the same fate as Trey." Ward paused before continuing.

"As you might expect, the kid was scared half to death. It was nearly a week after the murder that he showed up here wanting to talk to me. He had no one else to turn to. He's a kid whose been on the streets most of his life. Dad's in the pen for drugs and he hasn't seen his mother in five years. He's in my care now, for his own safety, but that won't go on forever."

"The case is closed", said Tanner. "Omar Stallings is in prison. What's the risk for this kid now?"

"Well, Mr. Tanner, you see Omar was not alone that night. He was apparently working for another man who showed up at the warehouse where my son was murdered. Devin knew Omar, but he had never seen the other man. All he knows is that Omar called him Elliott.

"Devin gave a statement to the police; when they picked Omar up, he confessed immediately. He denies that there was anyone else there that night. Says Devin probably imagined it because he was so scared. Both Omar and Devin took polygraph tests. Omar showed no deception; Devin's was inconclusive. The police followed up on the name, but came up with nothing. In the end, they bought Omar's version, but I don't."

Ward closed his eyes, breathing deeply to control his emotions. His jaw tensed, contorting his face. Thibodaux recognized the pain and glanced at Tanner, who nodded slightly.

Ward cleared his throat, swallowed, and continued, "I want that other man! He's the boss. He ordered the hit. Devin said Elliott told them both, as Omar tortured them, that they would die that night. But if they told him where the money was they owed him, he would kill them quickly rather than continue the torture. Can you imagine what that must have been like for my son?

"I want the man identified, located and brought to justice, one way or another. Will you take the job?"

Tanner could feel Thibodaux's eyes on him as he spoke. "Why did you choose us? What little investigative work we do is mostly missing persons and employee theft cases; even those are far from being a full-time business."

"Because the sheriff, Randy Jackson, has been my friend since we were in the Corps together at Texas A&M. I trust him and he said you believe in justice. He said you got involved in the case where Hobart Hansen's son murdered a young black girl, because you believed she deserved justice. I want that kind of man working on my son's case."

"Mr. Ward, that little girl, Danielle, was Thibodaux's niece. We both wanted justice, but it was personal for us; he's my friend. We're not crusaders who look for wrongs to make right. Besides, we never got anyone charged with Danielle's murder." Tanner sipped his coffee.

A hint of a smile showed when Trenton Ward began speaking. "I know how that case ended. Justice was served. Now maybe you just kept the pressure on until the Hansen kid couldn't take it anymore, but whatever happened, he answered for the murder. That's what I want for the man who ordered Trey killed. Name your price."

Tanner's gaze into Ward's eyes would have cowed a lesser man, but neither blinked. Finally Tanner broke the silence.

"We'll take the case. Here's what you can expect. We will try to identify this Elliott fellow and attempt to connect him to the murder of your son. No promises and it'll cost you one hundred thousand dollars plus any expenses we incur, regardless of the outcome, half up front, the balance when we bring you the true name of the guy you're calling Elliott."

"Done," Ward replied without hesitation. "The receptionist will have the check when you leave. Now, let me get the information I have for you."

Trenton Ward went to his desk, made a call during which he gave instructions to prepare a check and then removed a file from the middle drawer of the desk. He brought the file back to the conference table and slid it across between the two men.

"That file contains all the information I have, including where to find Devin. He's staying at my ranch outside Fort Worth. If you need anything else, let me know."

When Tanner and Thibodaux walked out, the receptionist handed Tanner an envelope with the check enclosed.

*****

As they drove out of San Antonio, Thibodaux spoke first, "That was strange. Sounded like maybe the sheriff told Ward that he thinks Hunter Hansen's death might not have been a suicide."

"Yeah, I got that impression too. Randy had some questions, but it wasn't his investigation and besides that, he was happy to see Hunter dead. Randy knew that was the only way he would pay for what he did."

"How'd you figure a hundred thousand? The most we've made on a job since we began doing this P.I. work is less than ten thousand," Thibodaux asked.

"He's a rich man. I didn't like him implying that he was hiring us to find and kill this Elliott character. No matter what impression the sheriff left Ward with, what we did to Hunter Hansen was because justice couldn't be served any other way. That's not likely to be the situation facing Elliott. But it should be fun trying to find him, knowing we're making fifty thousand each."

Both men knew what Trenton Ward expected of them. But they also knew that they would be guided by their own sense of ethics.

Larry Watts

Chapter 4

Finding Elliott and connecting him to Trey Ward's murder posed a few challenges. First, it would involve a drug operation, always a dangerous element regardless of other variables. Second, they doubted Omar would shed any light on the identity of the man he went to prison for. Third, they assumed Devin Blakemore was a street punk likely to be killed the moment he surfaced in San Antonio.

One of them might have to work his way into the drug supply ring Elliott controlled. Only Tanner would make contact with the witnesses Omar and Devin. Thibodaux would stay in the shadows until they determined if they would have to go undercover to find Elliott.

The next day Tanner drove to the Ward ranch southwest of Fort Worth. When he arrived, he wasn't surprised to be met by the ranch foreman, dressed like a character from a western movie— boots scarred and unpolished, spurs jangling when he walked, and jeans worn in the seat from hours in the saddle. He introduced himself as Buck and extended his hand.

"Mr. Ward told me you were coming. The kid is in that bunkhouse over there Let me know if I can help you with anything." He turned and walked back toward the corral where other cowboys were working with several horses.

Tanner knocked on the door. A young man with a sallow face, eyes sunken with dark shadows beneath them, peeked out.

"You're Mr. Tanner?"

"Just Tanner and I guess you're Devin." Tanner walked in and shut the door.

Both men sat down in well-worn, but comfortable wing-back, cushioned chairs.

"Start from the beginning and tell me your story from the time you met Trey or Omar, whichever was first."

Devin began without hesitation. "I've known Omar since I was fifteen. He used to be a street dealer in downtown San Antonio. I bought weed from him when I could afford it.

"Before long he put me to work and I fronted for him, making the transactions for him on the street. He had me accept all his deliveries too. He said if I got busted, it would just be a juvie rap and he would get me out. It worked twice before I turned seventeen. He showed up at the Child Protective Services, where they were holding me, and told them he was my uncle. They released me to him."

"Go on," Tanner said, settling back in his chair.

"Well, about a year ago I met Trey at a little bar off St. Mary's street. His family has money, but I don't think he got along all that well with his dad. I know Trey wouldn't have asked his family for anything. We started hanging together and I let him in on my deal with Omar. By then I was dealing mostly H and making some good change. I think Trey just liked being a part of the deal. He liked thinking of himself as a gangster.

"Trey loved to gamble. A couple of months ago, we came up short on the cash we owed Omar for the next delivery, because Trey was losing bets he placed with a bookie. Omar let us slide a month, but the next month we were robbed and didn't have his money again. That's when they killed Trey and I got away."

"What about the guy named Elliott," Tanner asked.

"Never saw him before that night. I knew Omar worked for some rich guy pushing dope, but the night Trey was killed was the first time I ever saw him. Omar had thrown his name around a couple of times before. Rumor is the guy's connected with all the political players and is untouchable, but I didn't recognize him as anyone I'd ever seen before. I hope I never see him again." Devin closed his eyes as if to get the image of Elliott out of his mind.

Tanner talked with him for another hour, taking notes, asking questions, and hoping to pick up bits of information to help identify Elliott. He then drove east toward Palestine, Texas. The landscape became more rural and traffic sparse. Tall pine trees bordering the highway leaned toward each other, reminding Tanner of a natural canopy. The lonely solitude was broken only when Tanner turned the radio on to a country music station. As darkness began to crowd the sunset, he found a hotel room at the edge of town. The next morning he would visit Omar at the Michael Prison Unit just outside Palestine.

*****

Tanner arrived at the prison unit and placed his car keys and identification in a bucket hanging from a rope on a guard tower known in prison lingo as a *picket*. A guard in the tower lifted the bucket where it would stay until his return.

Another guard escorted him to the office of Warden Terry Simon. Their friendship dated back thirty years when they both attended Milby High School in Houston. They spent an hour catching up on each other's lives before the conversation turned to Omar Stallings.

"He's got quite a reputation here with the other inmates," the Warden said. "Not many men will take a life sentence to protect a business acquaintance, but that's what they say Omar did. And nobody knows who that business acquaintance is. I doubt you'll get much from him, but you're welcome to try."

The warden escorted Tanner to a prisoner visiting room where a muscular, coffee-colored man sat shackled in chains to a large metal table. The man glared at Tanner through slightly squinted, dark brown eyes. Omar's scowl was as cold and impersonal as the drab grey room where he sat. Worn chairs, the same color as the walls, blended into the miserable prison room. Tanner sat down in the chair across from Omar, close enough to smell the strong odor of cheap soap from the prisoner's body. The warden moved one of the chairs to the wall and sat down.

"What if I could get you out of here, place you in a witness protection program and give you a new life in some other part of the world," Tanner asked bluntly, "are you interested in such a deal?"

Omar studied Tanner's face for a few seconds before responding. "All I got is time, boss, so it don't bother me if you want to talk, but there's no deals for me. I killed the kid and I'm doing the time. End of story."

Tanner stood before threatening, "I'm going to find Elliott. When I do, I'll pin at least one more murder on you and the next one won't be for a life sentence. You'll go to death row. If you change your mind, let the warden know. He knows how to reach me."

Tanner left the prison and began the long drive home. Along the way he phoned Thibodaux and updated him on the lack of progress during the last two days.

Chapter 5

The day after Tanner returned from interviewing Omar, he received a voicemail from Devin. In a tone of urgency and panic, Devin's message was, "*I saw him on television last night. Elliott! He's in Dallas. You've got to call me.*"

When Tanner called the number, Devin picked up before the first ring was complete, "Mr. Tanner? Is that you?"

"It's me, kid. Calm down. Now where did you see Elliott?"

"I watched the local news at ten last night. There was a story about the man who bought the Grand Prize winning steer at the State Fair.

"Part of the story showed a clip of him bidding on the steer at the auction. I saw Elliott sitting two rows behind him and to his right. I know it was him. I'll never forget his face." Devin's voice was even more stressed than when he answered the phone.

"Alright Devin, calm down. What television station was it on?"

"It was NBC because the *Tonight Show* came on right after the news, Devin answered. "You've got to get me out of here, Mr. Tanner. I would be safer in San Antonio."

Tanner knew that allowing Devin return to San Antonio would be a disaster. Within days he would be making contact with his old friends, a recipe for leading Elliott right to him. But Tanner kept the thought to himself.

"Let me talk to Mr. Ward and I'll get back with you. In the meantime, calm down. You're safe for now." Tanner hung up the phone and called Thibodaux.

"We've got a break on Elliott," Tanner began as soon as his friend answered the phone.

He related his conversation with Devin. When he finished, Thibodaux responded, "I'll get on the phone now and order a copy of last night's local news in Dallas. I'll get one from each broadcast, in case any of the other stations covered it also."

It was time to talk to Ward about relocating Devin. Tanner wouldn't let him return to San Antonio; he wanted to move Devin to a more remote location. His reasoning had less to do with Elliott locating him, than his concern that Devin would head for San Antonio on his own. He knew the kid wouldn't last long there.

The conversation with Trenton Ward didn't last long. Tanner told him about Devin spotting Elliott on the local news in Dallas. He also shared his concern about the possibility of Devin considering a return to San Antonio.

Ward agreed to move Devin to another of his ranches in the Davis Mountains a few miles from the town of Fort Davis. It was remote, with little chance that any of Devin's acquaintances would be in the area.

Ward assured Tanner his own people would move Devin to the new location. He also told Tanner a private airplane would be at his disposal if he felt the need to meet with Devin.

*****

Two days later, Tanner and Thibodaux sat in Thibodaux's living room reviewing the news clips from Dallas. Only the NBC affiliate had captured the image of the man Devin knew as Elliott at the cattle auction. But the single clip offered a clear depiction of his face and body. He would be easily recognized by anyone who knew him.

Dressed in a western-cut business suit, complete with bolo tie and black Stetson, Elliott presented an imposing figure, even seated in the bleacher-style arena set up for the annual auction. During the brief film shot, he gazed confidently at the arena where livestock paraded before the buyers.

But who was he?

Thibodaux worked with the digital file and isolated several still images of Elliott which he saved on a thumb-drive. The partners left for San Antonio to meet Trenton Ward. They felt certain that if Elliott was active in Texas' wealthy social scene, he would recognize the photos.

When they walked into the reception area, the greeting was much different this time. The shapely receptionist rose from her desk, walked to the massive double doors, and swung one open.

"Mr. Ward is expecting you."

Thibodaux spread copies of the several photos on the conference table.

"We think this is Elliott. Do you recognize him?"

Trenton Ward's first reaction was shock, but that expression quickly turned to puzzlement.

"Yes, I know him. That's Lamar Middleton. But he can't be the man that Devin says is a cold-blooded killer involved in narcotic trafficking. He's a billionaire, third-generation. His family owns convenience stores and fast-food restaurants throughout the southern United States."

"How do you know him," Thibodaux asked?

"We've known each other for years through business dealings. He served for a while on the board of directors of one of my banks in Dallas and made a play to become a minority owner in a Canadian hockey team I own. I can't imagine why Devin would think Middleton is Elliott."

"Do you know anything about his business? Has he had financial problems," Tanner asked?

"I don't have a clue about the health of his business, except that when an operation as large as his starts having problems, the rumors circulate pretty early, and I've heard none about him. He didn't have the resources to close the deal on the hockey team, but few others did either."

Thibodaux stood, "It's a place to start. We'll do some legwork, try to either rule him out or confirm he's our guy, but Devin's word on this is pretty convincing. We'll be back in touch."

"Oh, by the way, Tanner, Devin has been relocated. If you need him let me know. I'll fly you out to Fort Davis. If you've never been there, you'll love it; it's like stepping back into the old west." Ward's voice softened, "I used to take Trey there. He would swear he could feel ghosts of Apache Indians in those mountains." The emotion was evident on the father's face as he nodded good-bye and turned back to his desk.

Larry Watts

Chapter 6

Tanner and Thibodaux spent most of the next day side-by-side at their computers. The two agreed Thibodaux would begin a search of news stories mentioning Lamar Middleton. Tanner, in the meantime, conducted an on-line research of lawsuits associated with Middleton as well as other public information regarding his business and personal life.

After two intense hours, they took a break to compare notes. Thibodaux discovered several articles in various newspapers across Texas as well as a few in Louisiana, Oklahoma and Florida. Most of the stories centered on openings of new fast-food or convenience-store operations by Middleton Enterprises over the previous twenty years. A cluster of articles in the Dallas Morning News from the previous six years detailed a legal battle between Lamar Middleton and his two siblings, Theresa and Stephen, over control of the company all three jointly inherited.

Tanner spent the first hour trying to connect the names Elliott and Lamar. He learned Lamar had no middle name and was unable to establish any other connection. Theresa Middleton, on the other hand, was married to Charles Elliott for a short time in the 1980's. He also came across information about the legal dispute. Lawsuits and counter-suits filed by all three parties, before a settlement was reached.

The terms called for Lamar to assume ownership of most of the company's fast-food operations while his siblings kept the convenience stores. According to the agreement, Lamar maintained the name Middleton Enterprises, under which he continued to operate his businesses. Tanner found other lawsuits on file, but they involved mostly customer disputes, none of which raised any red flags.

Several hours at the computers helped create a detailed profile of Lamar Middleton. None of it pointed to the possibility of him being the mysterious and dangerous Elliott. They decided to call it a day's work and retire to The Dry Gulch Saloon for a beer.

When the two sat down at the picnic table beside the saloon, beers in hand, Tanner declared, "I think it's time to talk to Devin again. We need to know how to get into Elliott's circle. If we can find the right contact, you'll have to convince them that you can move a lot of dope for them."

"Now there's an interesting suggestion. You're the ex-cop, but you want me to infiltrate a dope ring," Thibodaux responded with the hint of a smile. "I guess I'm not too old to learn, but I never figured after retiring that I'd be acting out the part that Tim Roth played in the movie, *Reservoir Dogs.*"

"This deal won't be that intense," Tanner assured his partner. "We'll get you through, if it comes to that."

*****

The following morning, Tanner met Trenton Ward's corporate pilot at the San Antonio airport. The journey by plane to Marfa Airport shaved several hours of driving time Tanner would have faced. A car and driver awaited Tanner to take him into the Davis Mountains where Devin was located. The extravagant ranch house occupied a high plateau overlooking the town of Fort Davis, nestled in stunning mountain country. Although a lifelong Texas resident, Tanner never before visited the area. He would enjoy return trips under different circumstances.

When they arrived, he saw Devin waiting outside a small cabin. He looked better, Tanner thought. The fresh air and secluded life seemed to agree with him. Devin invited him in and the two men sat in a study with marbled flooring and finished cedar walls. This was a man's room, Tanner decided.

"How are things going, now that you are away from the big city?"

Devin grimaced. "Mr. Tanner, I really appreciate what Mr. Ward has done for me and

I've enjoyed learning a little bit about ranching, but I am awfully lonely out here. You know I grew up a city kid and the streets are where I belong, even if I don't survive to be an old man."

Tanner considered this for a moment before answering. "I imagine it's a big adjustment, but you've got to hang with us for a while longer. I need to find out who took Omar's place when he went to prison. Any ideas?"

"I've been away too long. All I know is that Jaime Rios was nipping at Omar's heels before all this happened. I'm sure he made a move to replace Omar, but I don't know whether he was successful."

"And who is this Jaime Rios?" Tanner asked.

"He's a street guy who's been selling dope, running whores, and doing whatever needs to be done for people like Omar and Elliott since he was sixteen-years old. He's getting close to thirty now and wants to move up the chain."

Devin shared everything he knew about Rios. When he finished Tanner was sure that Thibodaux could find Rios. Whether or not the man had achieved his goal of moving up, or if Thibodaux could work his way into Elliott's den, was still an open question.

Tanner said nothing about Elliott's true identity. "Just stick with the plan," he told Devin, "and you'll be back in the city in a few months."

In less than three hours Tanner took to the air again, stretched out on a comfortable, brown leather reclining seat. He looked around and reflected on the advantages of working for the wealthy, before drifting slowly into a dreamless sleep for most of the flight back to San Antonio.

Larry Watts

Chapter 7

When Tanner and Thibodaux met the next morning, they kidded with each other about the work they had taken on. Here they were; two old men, a soldier and a cop, having retired to the small town of Success, Texas, for a quiet life. Just yesterday, one flew half-way across Texas in a corporate jet, probably costing thousands of dollars for each hour of use. The other spent time preparing to go undercover into the dark streets of Texas' drug and crime culture. *Some retirement,* each thought as they sipped coffee.

Although simple in concept, the plan to infiltrate Elliott's criminal enterprise was potentially expensive. In order to make contact with Jaime Rios, Thibodaux would have to pass himself off as an insider of Louisiana's drug culture with a network of dealers in several northern Louisiana cities and towns.

If successful in making a business deal, he would begin purchasing a supply of drugs through Rios until the buy reached at least fifty-thousand dollars. At that point, he planned to propose moving up the chain to get to Elliott by offering to make a large purchase. Trenton Ward would have to front the money, maybe as much as a million or more. Tanner and Thibodaux also thought about something else. What would they do with the illegal drugs that were delivered?

Thibodaux set his coffee cup down. "This plan appeared to be simple when we started discussing it, but it has some serious issues. Do you have any ideas what to do about the dope we buy? I don't want to get busted and spend my senior years in prison."

"I'm not sure, but I have a friend who works for the DEA. I'll talk to him, tell him what we're doing, and see if he'll work with us on this. One thing I am sure of. No branch of law enforcement is comfortable with a *cowboy operation* like this, set up by civilians. Why don't you make the trip to see Trenton Ward and get his okay on fronting the money? I'll drive to Houston and run our plan by my friend."

*****

Two days later, Thibodaux drove to San Antonio and Tanner headed east toward Houston. Less than an hour after walking into Ward's office, Thibodaux left with assurances the money, when needed, would be wired to a bank account they owned. Thibodaux cautioned him that they could be talking about spending as much as a million dollars before they got to Elliott. Trenton Ward never hesitated. Once he decided to go after his son's murderer, no obstacle would stop him.

Tanner's assignment, on the other hand, proved a greater challenge than he counted on. Jack Ralston sat across the desk staring at his old friend.

"Tanner, if you were still at HPD would you get involved in a rogue operation like this?"

"I'm not sure, but I'd be much more likely to if you were the guy coming to me with it."

Ralston served as Special Agent in Charge, or SAC, of the Houston DEA office. He could accommodate his friend's request and would likely never be questioned. But no agency, local, state, or federal, ever knowingly allowed private citizens to set up such an operation that involved this volume of drugs and money. He also knew the kinds of problems inherent in these kinds of operations: money is lost or stolen, drugs disappear. Worst of all, those on the ground are sometimes killed. If Tanner was wrong, those involved would make enemies of one very pissed-off and influential billionaire from Dallas. It was a tough call, but the rewards could be enormous; Ralston made his decision.

"Tanner, I'll back you on this one, with some conditions. First, no buys without an agent working beside you covering your partner when he has the meetings. Second, Thibodaux clears all our background checks. Finally, every grain of dope is accounted for immediately and turned over to us."

"Done, Jack," Tanner replied almost too quickly. "We don't want to be in the narcotics business. We simply want to put eyes on the man called Elliott. Our hope is that once he's identified, you guys can make him for the dope and also tag him with the Ward murder."

The two old friends talked for another hour during which time Ralston phoned one of his agents, Terry Bishop, to come to his office. When he walked into the room, Tanner immediately thought, *Ivy League college boy,* but after Ralston made the introductions and briefed Bishop on the operation, the young agent asked sensible questions. Tanner decided to withhold judgment, at least until he knew Bishop better. Ralston made sure the two men understood his conditions explicitly.

As he cleared the Houston traffic, Tanner called Thibodaux. Each reported his success to the other and they agreed to meet early the next morning to begin the hunt for Jaime Rios in San Antonio.

*****

Connecting with Rios wasn't difficult. Thibodaux simply went to the bar on St. Mary's Street where Devin had told them he first met Trey Ward. When he asked about Rios, the bartender nodded to a man sitting in a corner by the back door of the bar. Thibodaux approached the table and sat down.

"Name's Thibodaux," he said, sizing up the other man.

Rios was not an imposing figure, but he had a face that made up for those short-comings in a man who wanted to control the streets. Acne scars covered both cheeks and a scar of another sort ran from the corner of his lower lip down to his throat. Staring at Thibodaux, he said nothing.

"I was told that if I wanted to do a certain kind of business in San Antonio, you were the guy to talk to," Thibodaux continued.

"And who would have told you that, *mi amigo?*" Rios sneered, his eyes still locked on Thibodaux.

"Omar," said Thibodaux without hesitation. "I've not met him, but we have a mutual friend spending time with him now."

For the first time, Thibodaux saw a reaction in Rios' expressions, although it was barely detectable.

"And what kind of business would it be that Omar told you about?"

"I need a new supplier. My friend who now resides with Omar can't deliver the goods from where he is. I've got a well-established business in Louisiana. I need uncut product. I'm not a street dealer," Thibodaux finished his pitch, hoping it sounded convincing.

"Meet me here tomorrow at four o'clock." Jaime Rios pushed his chair back and sauntered out.

Chapter 8

Thibodaux discussed the meeting with Tanner and they concluded Rios would probably attempt to check out his story. They didn't believe he would try to contact Omar directly, since, according to Devin, Rios had been trying to move in on Omar before he went to prison. It was a gamble, but they decided to take it.

They had purchased several items they jokingly referred to as *private-eye stuff.* Among the equipment was a body mike and remote receiver that would allow Tanner to monitor Thibodaux's conversation with Rios from outside the bar. If things went bad, Tanner could intercede on Thibodaux's behalf.

They drove separately to the meeting, with Tanner arriving thirty minutes early in a rented van. He parked across the street from the bar and moved to the back of the van so that he couldn't be seen. Thibodaux arrived a few minutes before four o'clock, parked and went into the bar where he found Rios sitting at the same table he had occupied the day before.

"Have a seat, *amigo.*" He paused while Thibodaux settled into a chair across from him. "So how much shit can you handle, assuming that I decide to do business with you?"

"My guys have been pushing over a pound a month and we could do more," Thibodaux replied. "Can you handle that kind of load?"

Rios ignored the question and reached into his jacket pocket. "I've got a gram for you and that's raw. It's also three hundred fifty bucks. You in?"

"Not enough. I got mouths to feed," Thibodaux countered. "If that's all you can do, I'll have to go elsewhere."

"Nobody said that's all I can do. It's all I'm going to do today! If you're in, put the cash under the ashtray, get up and go to the men's room. Look in the extra roll of toilet paper that's setting on the commode tank. Be back here next week, same time, same day."

Thibodaux counted out the money and grumbled about the high price tag. But he put it under the ashtray and went into the men's room. He found the package of heroin. When he exited the bathroom, both Rios and the money were gone.

When the partners returned to Success, Tanner called Terry Bishop and told him they made their first buy. Bishop was not happy.

"You know the deal Tanner. I'm supposed to be there when the deal goes down. Where's the junk?"

"We've got it here and there'll be another buy next week. We would have brought you in if we had known we were going to make the buy, but it went down too fast. It won't happen again."

Beginning with the next meeting, Bishop accompanied Tanner in the surveillance van to the meetings with Rios for the next three weeks. On the third week, Rios sold 10 grams of heroin to Thibodaux for three thousand dollars.

Before leaving, Thibodaux pushed his new found friend to provide even more. "Look, man, I can't make this trip every week for chump change. You're going to have to do better. I'll make a monthly run for a pound or I'll go to a New Orleans contact I've found. His prices are higher, but he'll supply what I need without the game playing. Your call; what'll it be?"

"I need to check with the man. That's a lot of shit and he'll have to okay the deal."

Rios had never mentioned anyone else before. The remark gave Thibodaux the opening he wanted. "I want to meet the man who makes that decision. Make sure he's here next week."

"Whoa *compadre*, you don't call the shots. Man's name is Elliott, but he won't be meeting you here." Rios stood to leave.

"You got anybody else in your stable who's turning a pound a month?" Thibodaux stared at Rios who remained silent. "I didn't think so. You set up the meet, wherever Elliott chooses; but I do my future business in *The Big Easy* unless I meet the man."

Thibodaux walked out, hoping that he didn't overplay his hand. He hoped Rios considered him a big enough fish for a transaction that would move him another notch up the ladder. Of course, Rios would have to convince Elliott to meet with Thibodaux.

*****

Thibodaux drove back to Success. Tanner and Terry Bishop followed in separate cars, watching closely until they were sure no one tailed Thibodaux. They rendezvoused at Tanner's home.

"Looks like we'll get to meet the man," Tanner said, as Thibodaux retrieved three beers from the refrigerator.

"Maybe," Bishop added, "but it will take a couple of meetings to buy the dope. Get your money together. Just hope the guy implicates himself in the deal during the conversation. I'd be surprised if he will ever allow himself to be pulled into an actual delivery."

All three knew they passed a milestone with today's meeting. Bishop left without finishing his beer, but Thibodaux and Tanner relaxed and drank another round as they discussed more mundane matters about life in Success, Texas.

*****

When Thibodaux entered the bar the following week, there were no customers in sight.

"You looking for Rios," said the bartender, "he said to meet him in the restaurant of the Riverwalk Holiday Inn."

Thibodaux left the bar. In the car, he phoned Tanner. "You heard the bartender, I assume?"

"Yeah, we got it. Bishop's already on the way. He'll set up in the hotel lobby. I'm going to try to find a place where I can monitor your mike. Be careful." Tanner sounded tense.

A portion of the restaurant's seating area was open air next to the San Antonio River that flowed through downtown San Antonio. There was a wide sidewalk between the seating and the concrete bulkhead that allowed tourists to walk at the water's edge.

Thibodaux spotted Rios sitting at a table by himself. As he walked toward the table, he spotted another man, whose image he had seen on a television news clip, walking along the Riverwalk away from the restaurant.

Larry Watts

Chapter 9

"Sit down here, *mi Amigo*," Rios greeted Thibodaux, gesturing toward the chair across the table from him.

"Where's the man," Thibodaux asked, not revealing he'd already spotted him strolling along the Riverwalk.

"You don't need to meet him. He sees you. If he tells me it's cool, then we'll arrange to get you the product," Rios replied.

"I don't meet him, we can't do business. I'm a guy who's bringing a lot of green to the table. Show me some respect or I walk." Thibodaux sensed there would be no meeting.

"Wait here," Rios ordered. He turned and headed for the hotel lobby.

Thibodaux saw him pull a cell phone from his pocket and dial a number. After what appeared to be a short conversation, Rios ended the call and returned to the table.

"He's going to try to come by, but it will be a while. While we wait, I'll buy you a beer, no?" Rios signaled the waiter.

Soon, Thibodaux felt the presence of someone behind him. A voice said, "Jaime, it's been a long time. How are you?"

The man moved around Thibodaux's chair and extended his hand to Rios. As he experienced his first close-up contact with the man Devin knew as Elliot, Thibodaux felt a sensation of being in the presence of evil. Rios shook hands with the man.

"Mr. Scott, it's good to see you. Why are you in San Antonio?" Rios asked.

"I had some business here. I'm flying back this afternoon and was leaving for the airport, but I saw you sitting here and wanted to say hello."

"Meet my associate, Mr. Thibodaux," Rios said as he nodded toward his tablemate.

The two shook hands and the man introduced himself as Jack Scott.

"Look, I've got to run. It was good to meet you Mr. Thibodaux. Jaime, call me soon." With that the man excused himself and left the hotel.

Thibodaux sipped his beer as he attempted to figure out what was going on. The man who just left the table was Elliott, but he and Rios had made it appear to be a chance meeting.

When he finished his beer he addressed Rios again, "Look, I don't have all day. Is Elliott coming or not?"

"You just met him. Now do you want to do business or not? You tell me when you will have the money and I will bring the product."

"That's it? The man doesn't talk?" Thibodaux chastised himself for not calling Elliott's hand at the table.

"Look, my friend," Rios voice had turned deadly cold, "Elliott wanted to put eyes on you to see if he might know you. He didn't, so he's okay with doing business. Because you whined about meeting him, I had him come to the table. No more discussion. Do you want this thing or not?"

Thibodaux knew the meeting wasn't going as planned, but he had no choice but to set up the buy. After a brief discussion, he and Rios agreed to meet again at the bar on Saint Mary's Street three days later. Rios would bring a pound of raw heroin and Thibodaux seventy-five thousand dollars.

*****

The caravan back to Success from the meetings in San Antonio was becoming routine. Tanner and Bishop alternated between leading and following Thibodaux's car to make sure he was not followed. Once again they gathered in Tanner's living room.

"This isn't going the way we want," Tanner began. "We know that Lamar Middleton is Elliott, but we don't have anything to link him to the drugs. He's a smart man."

"He is smart," Bishop conceded. He turned to face Thibodaux. "Do you realize that you just set up a buy of a pound of raw heroin? It sometimes takes years for an undercover agent to accomplish that. We'll take Rios down after the deal is made. This is a big one, with or without Elliott."

Tanner's face reddened. "Wait a minute. We've got a job to do that includes putting Middleton behind bars. If you close us down after one big buy, we'll never make a case on him."

"That's not exactly true," Bishop countered. "We got good surveillance photos of Middleton with Rios. You can take that to local police and ask them to open the Trey Ware murder case again. They are more likely to believe the witness now, Devin Blakemore, isn't it? The connection between Middleton and Rios, Omar's replacement, is hard to ignore."

"I'm going around you, Bishop." Tanner's anger was evident in his voice. "I'll call Jack Ralston. We're not going forward with this deal if you plan to take Rios down now."

"Look, you can call Jack and tell him your opinion. You know what I think? You guys are playing cops and robbers with a rich man's bank account." Bishop rose from his chair and left without another word.

Tanner got on the phone with Jack Ralston, before Bishop reached the city limits of Success. He related the conversation to Ralston who told him he would discuss it with Bishop when he returned.

"But, Tanner, I went out on a limb to work with you on this. I expect you and Thibodaux to be at that meeting and make the buy," Ralston insisted.

Both Tanner and Thibodaux translated the conversation with Ralston to mean that there would not be an arrest at the meeting. They made arrangements for Trenton Ward to transfer the money into their account in order to buy the drugs. Three days later, Bishop, Tanner, and Thibodaux were on their way to San Antonio to make the buy from Jaime Rios.

While Lamar Middleton visited Oklahoma City to attend a press conference for the opening of a new restaurant, Rios took care of some unfinished business for him. Mikey Jackson lay dead in a hay field on the outskirts of San Antonio's south side. After all these months, Middleton still considered Mikey a loose end.

Larry Watts

Chapter 10

When the three men met at Tanner's home before splitting up to head for the meeting with Rios, little conversation took place. Tanner and Thibodaux assumed Bishop didn't like being overruled on making an arrest today and was angry about it. Bishop, however, knew this was likely his last association with the two private eyes. Rios would be arrested today.

*****

When Thibodaux entered the bar, everything was just as it had been the first time he met Rios. He sat at the same table alone and no one else was in the bar. Thibodaux speculated Rios might be the bar's only patron.

As he sat at the table, Rios welcomed him, "*Amigo*, today starts a new relationship. Did you bring the cash?"

Thibodaux reached into the back pocket of his jeans and removed a thick manila envelope. He tossed it on the table in front of Rios.

After briefly opening the envelope and peeking inside, Rios said simply, "Go out the back door. There is a canvas bag setting on the garbage can to the right of the door. I will see you in a month." He then rose from his chair and left through the front door.

Thibodaux found the canvas bag exactly where Rios said it would be, took possession of it, and walked to his car. On the return trip to Success, he called Tanner.

"Everything smooth with you and Bishop?"

"Yeah, but Bishop wants you to pull over at the rest stop just outside the city limits. He wants to get his hands on the dope."

A few minutes later, all three men pulled into the rest stop. Bishop and Tanner got into Thibodaux's car; Bishop sat in the passenger's seat and Tanner in the back.

When Thibodaux handed the canvass bag to him, Bishop reached into it and tore a corner off the package it contained. Satisfied, he simply told Thibodaux, "We'll be in touch," as he exited the car.

The two partners sat for a moment before Tanner commented, "I don't like what just happened. Something has changed with Bishop and I don't think it's because he was overruled by Ralston."

Tanner got back into his car and the two returned home. An hour later, they both understood why Bishop had acted strangely as they watched the latest "breaking news" about the arrest of a major drug dealer, Jaime Rios, in San Antonio by the DEA.

Tanner jumped on the phone with Jack Ralston minutes later screaming into the receiver, "What the hell have you done, Jack? You told me you would handle Bishop."

"Calm down, Tanner. I told you I would talk to him. I did and he convinced me that he was right. I helped you as much as I could, but we don't do homicide investigations and getting a pound of raw heroin off the streets while arresting the bad guy *is what we do!*" Ralston was not apologetic.

"What about Thibodaux? Don't you think they'll come after him now? Middleton doesn't let anyone double-cross him."

"Calm down, Tanner. We told Rios that we'd arrested Thibodaux as well and that the first one to give us information on the drug trafficking will get the best deal. Your partner should be alright."

When Tanner ended the call, he immediately rang Thibodaux, "Let's have a beer at the Dry Gulch and talk about our case."

Ten minutes later, they sat in a corner of the bar, Tanner nursing his bruised ego and Thibodaux thinking of their next move.

"We could always handle this like we did the Hansen case," Thibodaux finally broke the silence.

Tanner's face revealed the shock at his friend's words. "We did that for some very personal reasons. This case is nothing more than a job. If we handle it like Hansen, we're nothing more than paid assassins. You can't be serious."

"I'm just considering the options, friend. Your police background causes you to be comfortable with playing by the rules. I understand that.

"But my time in the Middle-East taught me to figure out how to accomplish the mission. There were no rules. I'm just saying that the idea shouldn't be off the table, along with any others, of course." Thibodaux smiled slightly and reached for his beer.

*****

The following morning Tanner temporarily dismissed the discussion that had troubled him throughout the night, when he received a phone call from his friend, Warden Terry Simon. "Tanner, your friend Omar Stallings wants to talk to you. He asked the night-shift captain to get the message to me first thing this morning. Any idea what changed his mind?"

"Do the inmates have access to television news on your unit? If so, I may have an idea. I'm on the way. Can I see him this afternoon?" Tanner was already out the door.

"Yeah, they can watch the news in the day room if that's what they vote to do. You see, we run a democratic program up here when it comes to watching television," Simon laughed. "Come on. I'll get you in with him when you get here."

*****

Tanner called Thibodaux, told him about the call from the warden, and that he was on the way to Palestine. Thibodaux had already begun a much more thorough background check of Lamar Middleton, aka Elliott. The two men agreed to meet the following morning.

When Tanner arrived at the prison about two that afternoon, Terry Simon was waiting for him at the gated front entrance.

"This is some reception, having the warden, no-less, meet me at the front gate." Tanner smiled and shook hands with his friend.

"I just wanted to let you know before you go in that we are already hearing inmate scuttlebutt that something big is coming down involving Omar. We don't know what it is, but I'm sure it's connected to the reason he wanted to see you." The warden's face was solemn.

Tanner told him about the arrest of Rios and how he believed it could be tied to Omar. A few minutes later Tanner sat across from the inmate. The Warden again took a chair against the back wall, this time with an even keener interest in Tanner's conversation with Omar. The rumors circulating through the prison population could be an indication of potential violence either perpetuated by Omar or against him. The Warden hoped to glean some information that might forewarn him.

Chapter 11

Tanner couldn't read anything from Omar's expression. The convict sat impassively staring at Tanner.

Tanner believed he was in a more powerful position than during the first meeting. He wanted Omar to accept that power shift. Both men allowed the silence to fill the room.

"What do you want to talk about Omar? Has something changed?"

"Tell me the deal you'll get for me. Can you get me out of here? Can you have me relocated with a new identity? Can you get me immunity for anything else I might have done?" The questions were rapid-fire and to the point.

Tanner had years of experience negotiating deals with crooks. Despite being in his comfort zone, he realized he lacked the authority to offer any deals now.

"For what?"

"I thought you wanted Elliott. I can tell you who he is and I can lay out his drug operation."

"I know who Elliott is, so that's worthless information. I think we're going to have a very cooperative witness soon in Jaime Rios, who'll be more than willing to tell us about the drug operation when he pleads to his latest arrest for selling heroin. You did hear about that, didn't you?"

Tanner smiled. "So the only thing you have that I want, is enough information to put Mr. Lamar 'Elliott' Middleton away for the murder of Trey Ward. You got that for me, Omar?"

For the first time, Omar's body language betrayed him when he realized he had waited too long. His shoulders slumped nearly imperceptibly and his eyes narrowed. Tanner knew he had him.

"I could give you Elliott on the murder and on worse things than that," he said, still failing to acknowledge that *Elliott* was, in fact, Lamar Middleton.

"What could be worse than murder," Tanner asked, noting a hint of desperation in Omar's voice.

Omar's shoulders straightened again. "You tell me what the deal is for me. I'll give you a murderer, a pedophile, and a drug dealer, all wrapped up in one person, but nothing else until I have the deal."

Tanner concealed his surprise. Nothing he and Thibodaux uncovered even hinted at such a secret about Middleton.

He spoke slowly but deliberately, "Understand that I can't give you the deal. It will have to come from the Bexar County District Attorney for your state charges and from the DEA for the drug dealing. You give me enough to take to them and I'll have representatives from both agencies back here to sign agreements as soon as I can. If I can't make it happen, nothing you tell me will be used to make a case on Middleton."

Tanner impressed Omar at their first meeting. Omar found two other inmates who knew Tanner from Houston. One of the two was in prison as a result of a Tanner investigation. Both inmates agreed. Tanner was a sorry cop just like all the others, but had a reputation for keeping his word.

He decided to gamble that Tanner could deliver. "Lamar Middleton is Elliott. He uses that name because most of the people in my business don't have but one name and nobody asks.

"He's never been arrested for messing with kids, or even investigated, but to keep that from happening, five of them have been buried. They'll all be missing children reports from the Dallas area. I only know a first name on one of them. That was the first one I saw. Elliott called him Ronnie.

"I been dealing dope and running the streets since I was thirteen. I met Elliott when I was about sixteen and he was in his twenties. He was donating money to a runaway shelter in San Antonio and I was always hanging around there selling dope to the runaways.

"I started hearing about him meeting some of the boys away from the shelter and taking them to his ranch. Talked to one who said Elliott would give them money and dope to do tricks with him. Weird stuff; he liked to be tied up and spanked; then he'd want to have queer sex with them.

"I never went for any of that shit! But some of them told him I sold dope, so he approached me. He asked me to go to his ranch with him. I told him I didn't do that weird shit, but he said he had a business deal."

Tanner interrupted Omar. "Where is his ranch located?"

"The one he took all the boys to was in the Davis Mountains. He's got others though, one west of Fort Worth and another down south somewhere.

"Anyway, he started fronting the money for bigger dope deals, until finally I was running a pretty good operation. I'd meet him at one of the ranches every few months.

"I got there one Monday morning and he was fit to be tied! Said there'd been an accident and he needed some help. I went to the barn with him and there lay Ronnie on the floor. Looked like he was asleep, but he wasn't. He was dead! There was a bullet hole behind his right ear.

"I'd seen Ronnie around the ranch before. Elliott said not to ask any questions, just help him get rid of the body. We buried him out in a pasture."

Once Omar had decided to trust Tanner, he didn't want to stop talking. Tanner again interrupted, "What about the Trey Ward murder? Why'd he want him dead?"

Omar looked away for a moment. "That was partly my fault. I let them boys skip a month and then they were too far behind to catch up. One thing Elliott won't let anybody do is beat him out of money. Even if they'd had the money with them that night, he was still going to kill them. Otherwise, he thought people would think he's weak."

Tanner sat back and listened to Omar talk for another forty-five minutes without interruption. He knew of two other boys who were murdered by Elliott at the ranch when they threatened to tell the director of the shelter what he was doing. Omar suspected that two others who never returned to the shelter were also victims.

Tanner finally stood as Omar seemed to run out of words. He told Omar that he would make an appointment to try to make a deal for him tomorrow and then he left. As he and the warden walked to the gate, they were both sure there would be a new inmate coming soon, a very wealthy one. Tanner thanked the warden and drove home.

Larry Watts

Chapter 12

Tanner and Thibodaux called Jack Ralston first. He agreed to meet them in San Antonio when they arranged a meeting with the Bexar County District Attorney. Ralston sensed the importance of the meeting and told them that he would ask the U.S. Attorney from Houston to accompany him.

An hour later, things were in place to take down Lamar Middleton. Finally, the two friends sat back in their chairs and relaxed.

"By the way, Thibodaux, I haven't asked if you had any luck with the research on Middleton."

"I didn't think I had anything important until you filled me in on his sexual perversions with little kids." Thibodaux shook his head in disgust. "Some of his trips may confirm his sexual appetites."

Thibodaux reached into his briefcase, pulled out a manila folder, and removed a sheet of paper. He handed it to Tanner.

"You'll see there that during the last six years, Middleton has made a dozen trips to Thailand and ten to Brazil. When I first saw that, there was no red flag. Other than one trip to Germany, those were the only out-of-country trips he's made in more than eight years. But when you came back with this new information about his interest in young boys, I finally snapped.

"Thailand and Brazil are two of the most widely recognized destinations for Americans wanting to engage in child sexual exploitation. We'll have to dig deeper into his itinerary for each trip, but on the surface, that appears to answer the question of why he traveled to both locations."

Tanner studied the paper a little longer before replying. "Good work, man! I'm not sure I would have put it together. We may have good news for Trenton Ward after our Thursday meeting."

Thibodaux, always methodical, suggested they review their evidence. They listed both Devin and Omar as witnesses to Trey Ward's murder. Although Omar pulled the trigger, both believed Middleton's presence should be enough for the D.A. The rest was circumstantial. But they believed it should be sufficient enough to confirm that Middleton spent time at the shelter and maybe even that he took boys to his ranch. His trips out of the country would require some expensive detective work, unless the U.S. Attorney took over the investigation. Still, they were cautiously optimistic.

On Thursday Tanner and Thibodaux drove to the D.A.'s office in San Antonio for the meeting. With everyone in place around the conference table, they laid out the story and the evidence against Lamar Middleton. When they finished the presentation and answered questions, the U.S. Attorney and D.A. agreed to offer Omar a deal.

Once the meeting ended, Tanner and Thibodaux drove to Trenton Ward's office and told him what they learned and about the meeting.

Thibodaux suggested they could attempt to locate some of the victims from the shelter, but it was best to let the local D. A. pursue those leads.

When Thibodaux finished, Ward asked a simple question, "What is Middleton likely to get in terms of punishment for all these crimes?"

"We don't predict what the system will do," Tanner said, not surprised by the question. "As we said when we first met, we have identified Elliott and we have connected him to the murder of your son. The rest is out of our hands."

"Don't wait on the D.A. Try to find a victim who survived," Ward said.

*****

Since Ward's plane was available, Tanner decided to fly back to the ranch and talk to Devin again. Thibodaux traveled with him this time. The undercover operation was over. No reason he shouldn't sit in on the interview.

Once at the ranch, they found Devin thriving on hard work and clear skies. He looked happy to see Tanner, but appeared cautious when it came to Thibodaux. Tanner asked him about the shelter, if he knew any of the boys who had lived there, and if Devin knew of any who had disappeared.

"I know the place you're talking about," Devin said. "I didn't hang around there much; Omar always recruited some kid who was staying there to push his product.

"The only kid I remember disappearing was one I knew before I ever got into all this. He went to middle school with me and then I saw him on the streets after I was selling for Omar. His name was Tony Mendez. I didn't see him around for a while. Omar told me he had gone out west to some ranch. I don't know if he disappeared or just went away."

Tanner thanked him for the information.

"Do you think I'll ever get to go back to San Antonio?" Devin asked.

"Nothing is forever, Devin. Relax and enjoy this time. We'll let you know as soon as we can," Tanner answered.

*****

Devin's information proved valuable. A little research and some help from a San Antonio police detective Tanner knew filled in the blanks about Tony Mendez. His real name was Anthony

Mendez. His parents lived in south San Antonio. Two days later, Tanner and Thibodaux drove to their home.

When they arrived they found it to be a small frame house, with a well-kept yard. The home was unique because many of the homes on the street needed paint, had old cars on blocks setting in yards, and weeds covering much of the landscape.

A man answered the door.

"Mr. Mendez?" Thibodaux asked.

"I'm Tony Mendez."

"We are private detectives and we're trying to locate your son. I assume his name is Tony, Jr.,"

"Why do you want to see my son?" Mendez asked. "He hasn't talked to anyone since the accident."

Mendez invited the two men into his house and explained his son had suffered a brain injury while working on a ranch. He said Tony accidentally shot himself while mounting a horse with a rifle in his hand, wounding himself in the head. A deputy sheriff patrolling the area found the boy.

The owner of the ranch had later contacted the Mendez family and provided funds to care for their son. The benefactor's name: Lamar Middleton.

"Can we see your son," Tanner asked. "We'd like to show him a couple of photos and see if he might recognize either man."

"I don't think you understand, Mr. Tanner. My son stares vacantly into space. He won't respond to your questions, but you can come to his room and see for yourself."

Mendez led the two men down a short hallway to a bedroom. Sitting in a wheelchair was a young man who appeared to be in his late teens. Thibodaux sat on the bed next to him and spoke. Tony registered no response to the voice.

Tanner held a photo of Omar in front of Tony, but he didn't respond. Tanner then pulled a second photo from behind the first; a photo of Lamar Middleton. Tony's reaction was quick and anguished. He began emitting guttural sounds and moved his upper body as if trying to back away from the photo.

"I don't understand," Mr. Mendez said. "That is a picture of the man Tony worked for. He sends us money every month to help with Tony's care. Why does the picture scare him?"

"We don't know," Tanner said. "But we are trying to find out."

The two men sat with Mr. Mendez for over an hour, but left with no better understanding of what happened to his son than when they arrived. The story of the accidental shooting didn't make sense.

During the drive back to Success, they concluded Middleton might have tried to murder Tony for some perceived betrayal, and that Tony had escaped after being shot. Luckily the deputy came along before Middleton could finish him off. So Middleton rewrote the story and acted the gracious employer helping a family whose son was injured while working for him. Tanner and Thibodaux were shaken by the possibility that if their theory was correct, the billionaire's callousness was epic.

Larry Watts

Chapter 13

Tanner and Thibodaux finished the Trey Ward murder case, or at least so they thought. They reported everything they knew to Trenton Ward. The District Attorney and the U.S. Attorney traveled to the prison, met with Omar Stallings, and made a deal with him to testify. A warrant was prepared to search for the remains of Ronnie on the Middleton ranch. The young man had now been identified tentatively to be Ronald Allen Copeland, a fifteen-year-old from the Corpus Christi area. Authorities planned to take Omar to the Middleton ranch to help pinpoint the site.

On the morning before the warrant was to be signed, a well-known criminal defense attorney from Dallas, McNeil Masters, showed up unannounced at the Bexar County District Attorney's office. He insisted upon speaking directly to the District Attorney. When he was ushered into Paul Wainwright's office, he had an amazing story to tell.

"Mr. Wainwright, I have a client, Mr. Lamar Middleton, who has information on a murder, maybe more than one, that occurred on his ranch in the Fort Davis area. He was just made aware of this. The information he has is that the boy who was murdered was abducted from a boys' shelter in San Antonio. He was taken to Mr. Middleton's ranch and killed by a man he hired occasionally to work for him. The man's name is Omar Stallings, but the name he used when he worked for my client was Oscar Jackson."

Masters went on to tell the District Attorney that an employee of the ranch who witnessed the murder contacted Mr. Middleton and, in a conscience-cleansing conversation, revealed that Omar Stallings abducted the young man and took him to the Middleton ranch, where he sexually abused the youngster before murdering him. The witness also told his boss Omar threatened to kill him if he ever told what he had seen.

The criminal defense lawyer provided D.A. Wainwright with the name and contact information for the witness as well as his client's contact information. He told Wainwright to channel all communication with his client through him. He also said Mr. Middleton would cooperate voluntarily with efforts to find the remains on the ranch.

Two hours later, Warden Terry Simon, informed the District Attorney and U.S. Attorney that Omar was stabbed to death while working in the prison laundry. Simon called Tanner with the same information.

Tanner spent much of the afternoon on the telephone. Jack Ralston also called Tanner when he learned about McNeil Masters visit to the District Attorney's office.

"This entire case just unraveled in a matter of a couple of hours," Ralston told Tanner. "The only thing left is the dope case on Rios. We're checking this witness out who is supposed to have seen Omar killing the kid. But he'll be one of Middleton's flunkies. He may get a short sentence for not reporting the crime when it happened, but with Omar dead, his story has no holes. I'm sure Lamar Middleton will see that he is well compensated for his time."

*****

Tanner drove the short distance to Thibodaux's house. He found his friend cleaning a saltwater fishing rig in his backyard. The two men were planning to spend a few days relaxing along the coast of Galveston, and wanted to leave in a couple of days.

"You may as well put the fishing rig away. There's been a new development in the Ward case."

Tanner told Thibodaux about the phone calls and the death of Omar Stallings.

"I haven't called Ward yet. Thought I might leave that up to you. But you can bet he's going to want some more legwork done."

They went inside to make the call. Neither was surprised by Trenton Ward's reaction, "Son-of-a-bitch is going to walk without so much as a slap on the wrist. Can you guys meet me at my office tomorrow? I want to plan what we can do to see that he doesn't walk away from my son's death untouched."

After Tanner and Thibodaux agreed to meet him the next morning, they sat down to talk about their next step.

"What do you think Ward wants us to do?" Thibodaux asked.

"I'm not sure, but this guy Middleton has no business on the streets. I can't forget the look of terror on that kid's face when he saw Middleton's picture," Tanner said. "I wonder how many more Tony Mendez's there are out there that we don't know about."

Thibodaux stayed silent for a moment and then spoke. "You *know* we can fix this. This guy needs to be taken out."

"I'm not a killer, Thibodaux. The deal with Hunter Hansen was different. He murdered your niece. I'm not sure I want to do it again, no matter how much justification there is. Besides, this one would be much more difficult. Lamar Middleton is not a drunk who passes out in his car at the end of the night like Hunter did."

Thibodaux leaned back in his chair. "Tanner, you are the expert when it comes to investigations and knowing how the justice system works, or doesn't work, as in this case. But when it comes to killing another man, I'm the better choice. Hell, that's what my job was before I retired. The U.S. Government needs killers just as much as it needs tax collectors. If we do this, I'll figure out the details and you can shoot holes in the plan based on your law enforcement skills."

Tanner rose to leave. "Let's see what Ward has to say tomorrow before we take that road. Maybe there's another option. But if we decide to take Middleton out, it won't be part of our discussion with Ward. We'll take the money we've made from him and anything else we do will just be a public service. See you tomorrow."

Larry Watts

Chapter 14

When Tanner and Thibodaux arrived at the offices of Trenton Ward, they were ushered into his office. But the place looked different. The wall at one end of the office opened up into what appeared to be a media room. Comfortable reclining chairs were scattered about, all facing a gigantic television screen.

"Gentlemen, I am going to ask you to indulge me for a few minutes. I have a couple of clips of video that I want you to see. Please be seated," Ward motioned to the chairs.

Tanner and Thibodaux sat down. The lights dimmed. Seconds later, a video flickered in the darkness focused on the life of Trey Ward. The video began when he was a baby and ended when he was a young adult. Thibodaux guessed the last shot was months before his death. He and Tanner were sure the presentation was no less than heart-wrenching for Ward, but it played until the end.

Then Ward stood up. "Thank you for watching that with me," said Ward when the video ended. "I realized that I asked you to seek justice for my son, but you never knew him. It may seem as if toward the end, we had lost him. But his mother and I never gave up on him. I didn't become a man until I was on my own and thought that a dose of the same medicine might be good for Trey. Now I wish I had kept a closer rein on him."

Ward's face had reddened. He swallowed and blinked, shook his head, and then, breathing deeply, turned to meet the eyes of Tanner and Thibodaux. "I hope what you've just seen helps you see him as a real person."

Stepping to the projector again, he continued, "After learning about the atrocities that Lamar Middleton committed against young children, I understand the pain I'm suffering from the loss of my son is no worse than that of others who have come into contact with the man.

"Now please indulge me again and watch the other video. Over the last several weeks I have had a documentary film crew interviewing and preparing this video about sexual abuse of children. Although you won't be able to see the faces of most of those on the video, several are from the shelter that Middleton and Omar were associated with. None of them have actually identified either man as being the predator, nor have any of them agreed to participate in any legal proceeding to help make a case against Middleton. In fact, neither man's name was revealed to the members of our film crew. I think you'll see why in some of the interviews.

"These young boys have been badly damaged. Some of them will never get their lives back; others may recover eventually. None of them want to relive the horror of sitting in a room with the monster responsible for raping and torturing them. They are also under the impression that this documentary was prepared for airing on a PBS channel. They have no idea that I am involved, nor why."

When the video began, most of the interviewees' faces were either blacked out or positioned to protect their identities. The ninety-minute documentary, as expected, proved gut-wrenching. More than one of the young men mentioned wealthy men who had abused them after gaining their confidence with gifts or exotic trips. Two of them talked specifically about going to a ranch several hours from San Antonio and suffering at the hands of a man whose entire personality changed once they were safely behind the walls of a compound built on the ranch site.

When the video ended, all three men sat silently for a while. Ward brightened the lights in the room slowly.

"Mr. Tanner. Mr. Thibodaux. Thank you for the work you have done on this matter. If you have more ideas about how I might assist you in ensuring that Lamar Middleton will be prosecuted for these or any of the other crimes he's committed, I'd like to hear them now."

Ward relaxed in his chair and waited. Neither man offered anything. But Thibodaux finally spoke.

"Mr. Ward, he's not going to be prosecuted for drugs, for the murder of your son or anyone else. He's smart. He's got money for great lawyers. And quite frankly, because of his wealth, in my opinion, some authorities don't want to go after him. The price for losing might be too high."

Ward nodded in agreement. "That's why I wanted you to see and understand who my son was. It's also why I wanted the two of you to see what the lives of Lamar Middleton's victims are like, that is, the victims who survived.

"I won't ask you to do anything else for me. I thank you for your service. If I can ever be of assistance to either of you, please let me know. Now I would imagine that you would like to get on with your day. Thank you for coming." He shook each man's hand firmly, then stood quietly watching their departure.

*****

As Thibodaux drove north from San Antonio, the two men were silent. Tanner appeared to have been deeply affected by the interviews with the victims of sexual abuse. Both men were thinking that at least some of those young men had suffered at the hands of Lamar Middleton.

After they were well out of the San Antonio traffic, Tanner spoke, "How would you suggest we do it?"

"I need to think on it, Tanner. It will have to be a little more sophisticated than the Hunter Hansen case." He looked across the car at Tanner. "It is the right thing to do though, I'm sure."

Larry Watts

Chapter 15

A week after meeting with Trenton Ward, the two men sat in Tanner's office to sip coffee and plan the death of Lamar Middleton.

"What have we become?" Tanner muttered, placing the coffee cup on a coaster beside his computer. He took a deep breath and released it slowly. Closing his eyes, he shook his head as if disapproving his own thoughts.

"When we took out Hunter Hansen, it was personal. We had tried everything to get the justice system to punish him and it hadn't worked. It wasn't difficult for me to rationalize that your niece, Danielle, deserved justice and we could give her that. But it's not personal at all with Middleton. Trey Ward shouldn't have been murdered, but he put himself in that position. Are you sure about this, Thibodaux?"

With fists clenched at his sides, Thibodaux met Tanner's gaze unblinking. "I think this guy is worse than my niece's killer. He's left a string of young kids with emotional scars they'll carry the rest of their lives. That's before you even start thinking about those he actually murdered. It's not about Trey Ward's murder. It's about an evil man. But you have to be able to live with your conscience and if you can't, I understand."

Tanner turned and stared at his computer screen for several moments.

"When we first worked together, I told you about a murderer who happened to be a judge's son. His last victim's name was Channing Scott. That's the little girl he was kneeling over when the police arrived. I could have kept her from being killed if, when I was pulled off the case of his previous murder, I had just been willing to speak up or handle him the same way we did your niece's killer. I admit, I thought about it then. Tell me your thoughts on Middleton."

"You're the detective, Tanner, and I don't want to insult your profession, but committing a murder undetected is probably easier than most people realize. Most people think the key is to avoid having suspicion focused on you. But a successful murder is one that the authorities never classify as murder, and instead assume they are suicides, accidents, or death by natural causes.

"Before we go into that, let me tell you the information I've gathered on Middleton. As you know, he owns a ranch in the Davis Mountains. What you probably don't know is that his ranch and Trenton Wards' have a common boundary. With all their other holdings, I doubt either man is even aware of this. Devin Blakemore has been staying less than a mile from Middleton's ranch home.

"I also managed to get some medical information on our guy. He's had some liver problems that may be the result of his battle over the years with alcoholism and drug abuse. He was in the Betty Ford Clinic a few years ago, about the time he was in the big fight with his siblings over control of the company. He apparently feared they would use his weakness against him and went there to blunt any accusations.

"He's a hunter and spends part of his time at the ranch camping out and playing the part of a cowboy. That's one of the things that may have attracted some of the kids he lured there."

Tanner's investigative skills kicked in and he interrupted Thibodaux. "How'd you get his medical information? Are there witnesses or a paper trail back to you on record searches about the location of the ranch or his hunting activities?"

Thibodaux smiled at his friend. "No, most of my training has been in avoiding being detected. I ran missions in Afghanistan where the first task was to locate a Taliban or Al-Qaeda leader hidden in a safe house. We had to find our guy without raising suspicion, figure a way to get within reach of him, then kill him and get away without detection.

"Often, simplicity is the answer. Mining a man's trash, both at home and the office, can often tell you more than the most sophisticated surveillance and computer checks. You know I've traveled to Dallas several times. It took only a few days to figure out when Middleton put his trash out, or more specifically, when his maid put it out.

"I learned his health insurance carrier, what items were charged on credit cards, the books he orders, and how much he pays in real estate taxes, just by looking through his garbage. The big prize, though, was a printout of all his usernames and passwords for bank accounts, social media, and everything else he does on the computer. Most people don't use paper shredders at home. When they update their records, they often just throw the outdated printed copy in the trash.

"I used a public library computer in several different cities to access his accounts. It's incredible how little information you have to provide a public library to use their computers, and before you ask, yes, the I.D. I used had a photo so dark no facial features were distinguishable and I made it on another public computer.

"Unless Dallas police solve a minor burglary of an insurance company's office where a petty cash fund was stolen, they'll never know that I hacked into Middleton's health insurance records while I was there. The petty cash theft made it look like a street druggie looking for enough money for the next fix.

"The information about Middleton's hunting activities at the ranch was pretty clear when I reviewed his purchases on-line and by American Express, but it also included a phone call to a local realtor in Fort Davis. I asked about ranches for sale and hunting leases. His was one on a list of four that I asked about. It's surprising how much information you can get in rural communities. And, by the way, I used the name Donovan Green and a burner phone with pre-paid minutes that I purchased from a convenience store thirty miles north of Austin. I busted it up and threw in the San Gabriel River after making the call."

"You've been a busy man," Tanner said, smiling at his friend. "I'm impressed with your talent. Now tell me how we do this and keep the law from believing it was a murder?"

"First, we make sure he dies on the ranch. Jeff Davis County has a sheriff and one deputy. The Sheriff may call in a Texas Ranger if he suspects foul play, but if it's a convincing accident or from natural causes, he probably won't. By the way, I ruled out suicide because there's nothing in Middleton's past that would indicate the possibility of suicide. In fact, he was diagnosed once as having a Narcissistic Personality Disorder. Narcissists have a very low tendency toward suicide."

Thibodaux then explained two detailed plans to take the life of Lamar Middleton. One involved poison that would indicate his liver problems caused the death, the other a hunting accident.

After an hour-long discussion of the pros and cons of each approach, the two friends decided Middleton would die accidentally. They both believed an accidental death would raise less suspicion in a rural community than a natural death. It would also avoid the necessity of pinpointing scientific conclusions about the body itself.

Tanner's indecision regarding the matter of serving justice with private retribution faded as they discussed details. With the name Channing Scott and the murder scene photos never far from his memory, Tanner easily rationalized the justice of what they were planning. Before she was killed, he investigated a previous murder and identified the judge's son as the killer, but he'd been pulled off the case before he got the chance to file charges. He didn't object. But the man struck again. Channing Scott lay dead with the murderer stooped over her when the police arrived.

Lamar Middleton, just as politically connected as the judge's son, and much wealthier, would pay for his behavior.

Chapter 16

With their fishing trip on hold, they spent the next two weeks preparing and discussing plans for the journey to Fort Davis and the Middleton ranch.

Tanner was amazed by Thibodaux's attention to detail in covering any possibility of linking the two of them to Middleton's death. The thought crossed his mind that he was lucky never to have investigated a crime planned by Thibodaux.

"When we make our trips to the ranch, we'll take my old pick-up truck. I have two fifty-five gallon drums that we can fill with diesel for fuel. By doing that, we won't have to stop at service stations where there may be surveillance cameras that capture evidence of our trip. We'll also use burner phones. We won't take our cell phones because of the GPS tracking.

"I did some research with satellite imagery on both the Ward and Middleton ranches. There's an old cabin, probably something that was used years ago, on Ward's ranch, not far from its border with Middleton's place. It appears to have a dirt road running to it from a county road. We can use that as our base if it's livable. If not, we'll sleep in tents. We don't want to advertise our presence there anymore than necessary."

Thibodaux stopped talking and gave Tanner time to digest it all.

"When do we leave and how long will we be there?"

Thibodaux smiled, "I thought this was a joint effort. You sound like a junior partner in this. No critique?"

"As you know, I did the planning on our first caper, so I figure this one's yours. I have to admit that I think you're better at this than I am though." Tanner noticed that his friend appreciated the compliment.

"Well, thanks for the vote of confidence. I think we leave Monday. We'll probably have to make at least three trips up there.

"This first trip will be to make sure we can get to and stay in that cabin, to hike into Middleton's ranch and find a suitable location for the accident, and to get a better understanding of the layout of his ranch house. When it's time to do the deal, we may get lucky and follow him to a campsite if he plans on a hunting trip; otherwise, we'll have to take him at the ranch house. That's a much riskier proposition, since he has ranch hands there all the time and might have guests as well."

"What about hunting companions," Tanner asked. "How will we separate him from them without being seen?"

"It's a good question that I don't have the answer to yet," Thibodaux said. "Maybe we'll figure it out when we see the layout. If not, when they actually go on the hunt, they're likely to be in separate deer stands with some distance between them."

*****

Tanner and Thibodaux had known each other for nearly five years. They had worked together, and before becoming partners, created one of the closest bonds two men can form; they had killed the man who murdered Thibodaux's niece. But they never spent much time on casual talk. This changed on their road trip to the Davis Mountains.

With Thibodaux at the wheel, they headed west from San Antonio on Interstate 10. Thibodaux peppered Tanner with questions about his years as a Houston police officer, his failed marriage, and whether his expectations from life had been fulfilled.

Tanner, on the other hand, wanted to know more about Thibodaux's years of growing up in a small Texas town where racial lines were still drawn, even years after desegregation. He asked about his friend's years in the Army as a Delta Force member, and found Thibodaux surprisingly open about his past.

Some aspects of Tanner's police career triggered mild depression at times. The death of Channing Scott; a horrible fire he discovered that claimed the lives of an entire family; including an infant; and the look of anguish on a little girl's face when he and his partner burst into a room where she was being raped by her step-father.

Thibodaux, at least on the surface, seemed at peace with all he had seen and done as a soldier who hunted and killed those identified as enemies of the U.S. Government. Tanner asked him about this ability to walk away from the past.

"When I was a teenager I was poor, black, and small. Some of my friends spent a lot of time complaining about the lack of opportunity for a black kid, or not having the advantage of wealth. Others became withdrawn when kids, black and white, picked on them and tormented them, because they were, like me, not yet fine specimens of manhood." Thibodaux smiled at the attempt at his own humor.

"I knew, though, that I would be destined to a life of misery in Success if I didn't put everything behind me each day and start my life as a new beginning. I trained my mind to forget the insults, empty stomach, and bullying I was sometimes subjected to. I trained my mind to be positive without even knowing what I was doing.

"When I went into the Army, I was soon being recognized for my competitive nature physically and my analytical approach to problem solving. I never considered the moral issues involved in killing a man who had been identified as an enemy. I just did my job. I take it from your question that you have difficulty doing that. I am probably a very lucky man for having been given that ability."

The conversation trailed off after a while, both men contemplating what they had learned about the other. Although a life-long Texan, Thibodaux never drove farther west than Kerrville. The miles and miles of huge wind turbines strung along the Interstate, with their massive propellers turning rhythmically in the breeze, impressed him. Tanner, however, traveled this route several times and took the opportunity to nap as the tires hummed over the concrete highway.

They left the Interstate and began the trek south toward Fort Davis. A spectacular landscape lay ahead as they wound their way into the mountains. During a heavy rain shower the truck's engine strained from the climb. Another month and all the greenery would be gone, but today they enjoyed a beautiful sight; two men, driving toward a destiny that ended in taking another man's life.

Once they passed through Fort Davis, Thibodaux studied the mountain terrain as he drove. Having driven military vehicles in the mountains of Afghanistan where virtually no roads existed, he easily conquered the twists and turns. Thibodaux glanced out the window in different directions and realized the opportunity that existed for creating a deadly hunting accident. First, however, they had to capture their prey without being seen.

With Tanner studying the map and helping navigate, they arrived at a deeply rutted road leading to the cabin. Tanner concluded there would be little reason for others to use the road, since it appeared to end just a few yards past the gate that would allow them onto the Ward ranch and access to the cabin. Thibodaux pulled to a stop at the gate. Tanner got out and found a rusted chain and padlock securing the gate. Within seconds he disposed of the lock with a pair of bolt cutters.

When they passed through the gate, the last days of Lamar Middleton's life began ticking away.

Chapter 17

By the time they unloaded their supplies from the truck, unrolled their sleeping bags and polished off a simple meal of tuna on crackers, it was time for bed. They would be up early in the morning, crossing onto the Middleton ranch to find a location to stage the accident.

Thibodaux had decided that the best opportunity would be to have their victim *fall* from one of the steep, rugged mountainsides to his death. As he waited for sleep to come, he considered the spot and where it should be in relationship to the Middleton ranch house. It could take a while to find the right location, since neither of them was familiar with the terrain.

Thibodaux awoke to the smell of freshly brewed coffee. Tanner stood over an old, rusty, Coleman camp stove. They agreed not to build any fires, but hot coffee in the morning was a must. The old stove would serve that purpose and posed little risk of disclosing their presence.

By six o'clock, each downed a cup of coffee and a boiled egg that Tanner prepared at home. The sun peaked over the eastern skyline when they left the cabin and hiked across the road onto Middleton's property.

They spent most of the morning climbing, starting at the southern base, climbing in a northerly direction, before finally reaching a mountain plateau no larger than a football field. The path had been rough and sometimes so steep that Thibodaux worried they would be forced to turn back and explore another route. But persistence paid off. From the north edge of the plateau, the view was spectacular, stretching for miles. A clearing was visible where a ranch house, corrals, and several outbuildings dotted the landscape. Middleton's ranch headquarters, they decided.

There was a single path down the north slope of the mountain. It was a well-traveled trail with a more gradual slope than the side they scaled. Close to the center of the plateau was evidence of a regularly used campsite, with a fire ring and cooking grate resting on two cinder blocks. But the most compelling discovery awaited at the western edge of the plateau. A sheer drop of more than a hundred feet before the mountain became less vertical. Giant boulders crowded the area. The incline appeared too steep to traverse. Both acknowledged it as the perfect location for their plan.

They sat for a few minutes on a small boulder at the edge of the cliff, winded from the climb, but satisfied with the result.

"I figured we'd be climbing all day to find the right location," Tanner said. "Our day has been a success and it's only one o'clock."

"Let's get back to the cabin," Thibodaux suggested. "There's nothing else to do until we know when Middleton will be here. We can start the drive back early in the morning."

They decided to take the northern slope back down the mountain, which, as they suspected, proved to be a much easier hike. After they reached the base they circled in a westerly direction. Once off the trail that led to the ranch house, they found the hiking more difficult. Heavy growth of pinyon, gnarly juniper trees, and a smattering of mesquite bushes slowed progress. At about two-thirty in the afternoon, they spotted the road to the cabin. Thirty minutes later they were back at Thibodaux's truck.

After a short rest, the two men filled the truck's fuel tank with diesel, the second time since leaving Success. As the darkness began to embrace them, before the full moon filled the sky with light, the two men sat on the tailgate of the truck and took a moment to enjoy the vastness of nature surrounding them.

"It's a long way to the big city," said Tanner. "I hate to spoil the purity of this place with what we're going to do."

Thibodaux chuckled. "*Ashes to ashes and dust to dust.* What we're going to do is more appropriate here than in the big city atmosphere of auto exhaust and industrial smokestacks. Death is natural. Wouldn't you rather die here than surrounded by heavy traffic, impersonal crowds of people, and the anonymity of the city?"

Tanner stood, "I guess you're right. It's time to turn in if we plan to be on the road early. I know you want to get back home and tap into Lamar Middleton's life on e-mail and social media again, so we can plan the next trip."

*****

The full moon helped guide their early departure, since they didn't want to use the car lights advertising their presence. They drove several miles from the cabin before turning on the headlights.

Their trip back to Success resulted in less conversation. Both men were lost in personal thoughts. The day's journey further sealed a friendship that would continue for years.

They pulled into the alley behind Tanner's home at six that evening and unloaded the remainder of the supplies. Thibodaux put the two unused 'burner' phones away to save for the next trip.

"I'll be traveling to San Antonio tomorrow," Thibodaux told Tanner. "I found a little bookstore downtown that has fifteen computers lined up along one wall for the use of guests. No sign in; no trace of who used them. I'll peek into Middleton's life on the information highway. There's nothing we can do until we see some indication he's headed to the ranch. Deer hunting season opens in six weeks, so I wouldn't be surprised if he made an early trip to get ready for the season. I'll let you know as soon as I have something."

Larry Watts

Chapter 18

The next morning Thibodaux arrived at the bookstore just after ten. He used the passwords and login names he'd retrieved from Middleton's garbage to log in to his e-mail. After scanning several messages, Thibodaux found the one he was counting on. The message, addressed to 'Middleton Ranch Manager' read: *Barton, I'll be at the ranch in two weeks. Let's make sure the deer stands are ready and check out the camp site. I want to spend some time with the kids while I'm there too. Opening week-end I intend to have a party for some of our friends. I'll be there on Monday, the 4th. Have someone at the Marfa airport to pick me up by noon.*

Thibodaux realized their opportunity might be sooner than he anticipated. The part about spending time with the kids raised his curiosity. He knew Middleton invited boys and young men to the ranch at times. This message sounded as if he was referring to kids who lived at the ranch. He printed the e-mail and would get Tanner's take on it later.

He found several other interesting e-mails, if for no other reason than learning more about Middleton's connections. Three e-mails went to the Governor, one to a U.S. congressman, and several to state senators, all seeking support for political issues. He found form letter responses from most. The Governor, however, sent a more personal reply, assuring Middleton of his support.

Thibodaux then checked Facebook, Twitter, and Pinterest accounts for Middleton. Although all three were active, it was obvious he didn't spend much time with social media.

Armed with the new intelligence, Thibodaux drove back to Success and to Tanner's home. The two men read the e-mail again and discussed the contents. Neither understood the reference to spending time with the kids.

"I guess we may find the answer when we go back there," Tanner said. "At any rate, it looks like this could all be over soon."

They made plans to repeat their previous road trip in ten days, arriving on Sunday before Middleton flew in on Monday. According to the plan, they would watch the ranch house from the campsite that they hoped Middleton was referring to in his e-mail. Once they detected movement toward their location they would conceal themselves just over the south rim of the plateau and wait for Middleton and his ranch manager to separate. When that happened, the accident would take place.

*****

The next week flew by. Thibodaux refilled the diesel barrels while Tanner bought more supplies. They repeated their previous routine of no lights, no fires, and meals from tin cans. With luck, they'd return home before the week's end. But Tanner bought enough food to last for ten days.

By Saturday evening both men were anxious to get on the road. They met for a beer at The Dry Gulch, to discuss the next morning's drive, and left the bar before ten. Thibodaux agreed to pick Tanner up at five the next morning.

The Sunday morning drive proved uneventful. Just outside of Ozona, Texas they pulled to the side of the road and pumped the tank full of diesel. Not a single car passed as they finished the task and got back on the road.

Thibodaux was mesmerized again by the electrical turbine windmills. Although not an enthusiastic environmentalist, he liked the idea that wind could be used to power homes and businesses. People like Trenton Ward and even Lamar Middleton were usually the economic force behind such ventures. But even with their vast wealth, they seemed to suffer the same personal and family problems of the poor and working class Americans. Money really couldn't buy everything a person wanted.

At five o'clock Thibodaux turned on to the dirt road leading to the cabin and drove to the gate. Tanner got out and opened it and confirmed that nothing had been disturbed, including the small thread Thibodaux insisted on running through the two ends of the chain to determine if someone opened the gate.

They followed the same routine as before, hopping on the tailgate of the truck to eat Spam sandwiches.

"We've got to wrap this up soon," Tanner joked. "All this canned meat is not good for my health. I can't remember the last time I ate Spam, probably when I was a kid."

"It was part of my diet when I was growing up," Thibodaux said. "Fried Spam, Spam and eggs, Spam sandwiches. There was no limit to my mother's innovation with cheap food. But to tell you the truth, I'm enjoying this sandwich."

Both men turned in by nine that evening. The following day would be a long one, spent crouched in the underbrush on the side of a mountain. Or it could be much more exciting and dangerous.

At 4:30 they both rolled out of their sleeping bags. Tanner made coffee and they ate boiled eggs before preparing to hike back up the mountain. Each carried a pistol; Tanner armed himself with a Glock 9 mm and Thibodaux a Colt .45 caliber automatic. They hoped their mission could be accomplished without the use of either.

With a better sense of the terrain, the trip up the mountain to the plateau went faster. At 10 o'clock they quietly peered over the brush at the campsite and saw that it undisturbed. They moved to the north edge, using binoculars to focus on any activity at the ranch house. It wasn't long before the realization sunk in that today would be the day.

Larry Watts

Chapter 19

Tanner spotted the four-wheelers first. They moved away from the ranch house toward the trail that would eventually lead to the plateau where Tanner and Thibodaux waited. Too far away to identify the riders, they assumed Lamar Middleton and his ranch manager, Barton would soon be joining them at the top of the mountain.

"Let's get back in position out of sight," Thibodaux said as he backed away from their vantage point.

They made their way back across the campsite to the edge and concealed themselves behind underbrush, with a view of the camp. Within five minutes, they heard the sound of the Honda engines as the two four-wheelers wound their way to the top of the mountain.

The vehicles bounced into the clearing, where both riders stopped their machines and climbed off. Thibodaux and Tanner recognized Middleton. The other man was about fifty years old. He looked tan and fit, suggesting someone who spent his time outside, engaged in physical work. The partners silently agreed that the man was the ranch manager. On the back of his four-wheeler were two large bags.

"I'm going to get some firewood gathered and prepare the campsite," Middleton said. "You take the deer corn down to the feeders and fill them."

The second man did as he was told without speaking. He boarded the vehicle and headed back down the trail within seconds. Middleton bent over the fire pit and moved some half-burned logs from the center. As he straightened his body, he looked up and saw Tanner staring at him from across the pit. He did not see Thibodaux standing behind him.

"Who the hell are you?" Middleton blurted. "How'd you get up here?"

Thibodaux spoke softly from behind him, "Just move over there," he said, pointing to the western edge.

Middleton wheeled around to face Thibodaux, his face masked in confusion. There was a hint of recognition.

Tanner grabbed Middleton's arm to move him toward the precipice. Still confused, Middleton allowed himself to be guided for a few steps before stopping and yanking free of Tanner's grip about ten feet from the edge.

"What the hell is going on? Get off my land."

A look of fear flashed across Middleton's face, as if he suddenly fully recognized Thibodaux. Both men grabbed his arms and shoved him over the edge of the plateau.

A long scream tore from his throat as his body plunged through the air for nearly fifty feet and hit headfirst on a large bolder. The body plummeted another fifty feet, and bounced off rocks and tree limbs. It came to rest across a large outcropping of rock, precariously dangling at the next level of rough mountainside.

Both men heard the sound of the returning Honda engine, when it topped the plateau. The driver pulled to a stop a few feet from where Tanner and Thibodaux were peering over the edge.

Thibodaux cried, "Are you Barton? Mr. Middleton fell over the side."

Barton was visibly confused by having returned to the campsite to find two strangers, but upon hearing that Middleton had fallen, rushed to the edge of the cliff. When he leaned out over the edge, Thibodaux shoved him. Unlike his boss, Barton dove nearly seventy-five feet before crashing against the rock edge. He bounced well past Middleton's body and came to rest nearly out of sight from above.

"Thibodaux. What the hell? He was just a ranch hand."

"We call it collateral damage," Thibodaux responded, "and when you think about it, you will know there was nothing else to do. Now let's get off this mountain and head for home."

Tanner stared for a moment as he realized his partner was right. They couldn't leave a witness. But they needed to work a bit more on the story.

"Did you bring the rope?" he asked Thibodaux.

"It's back there where we waited. What are you thinking?"

"Let's tie it off to something up here. Then we'll dangle it over the edge. We need to create a believable scenario for the investigators to consider. Middleton fell over and Barton tried to save him by repelling down the rope, slipping and losing his own life for the effort." Tanner turned and began preparing the scene.

After scrubbing any evidence of their presence, they left the mountain and were back at the cabin by 4 p.m. Both men were tired, but were aware of the urgency to get out of the area as soon as possible. An hour later they started the return trip to Success.

It was 2:30 the next morning when they reached home. Both men felt drained of energy and in need of sleep. And, both slept until noon the following day.

Although they figured the bodies wouldn't be discovered for several days, they were surprised when the news broke the following afternoon.

Chapter 20

Tanner called Thibodaux and invited him over for lunch. While sitting at the breakfast table, a San Antonio television station interrupted regular programming with an urgent report.

In a breaking news story, authorities in Jeff Davis County have found four young men, two of them adults, both seventeen, and two minors who are believed to be fourteen years old and appear to have been kidnap victims. They are telling investigators that they have been held captive for more than three months on a ranch belonging to billionaire real estate, restaurant, and convenience store investor, Lamar Middleton.

Additionally, authorities have found the bodies of two men, one of whom confidential sources within the Sheriff's Department tell us, is that of Middleton. The bodies were recovered on the steep, treacherous terrain more than one hundred feet from the top of a mountain on the ranch. Initial reports indicate that officials believe the deaths to have been accidental.

The young men, all previously reported as runaways by their families, have told the Jeff Davis County Sheriff that they were invited to the ranch as guests of Middleton, but were held captive after their arrival and sexually abused by both Lamar Middleton and his ranch manager, Trace Barton.

Stay tuned as we'll have more on this developing story.

The men stared at each other for a few moments before Thibodaux asked, "You alright with my having pushed the ranch manager over the side now, Tanner?"

*****

A month later, after the media focus began to diminish; Trenton Ward called Tanner and asked that he and Thibodaux drive to San Antonio where his airplane would be available to fly them to his ranch. When they arrived at the ranch Ward met them and invited them into his study.

"I want to tell you how much I appreciate your work. I could not have envisioned a better outcome."

"Mr. Ward, our work for you was done months ago," Tanner interjected. "As far as Middleton's recent misfortune is concerned, I'm afraid you'll have to thank someone else; if you're a religious man, maybe God himself."

"I understand," Ward replied, "but I also wanted to update you on the investigation. I'm not sure whether you are aware that the District Attorney in Jeff Davis County has officially ruled the deaths of Middleton and his ranch manager as accidental. He has determined that one or the other accidentally fell from the side of the mountain. The other, in an effort to save his companion, slipped and met the same fate.

"Of course, with the other revelations of what was going on at his ranch, neither man is viewed as a hero. Middleton's siblings refused to even comment on his death.

"There is one very happy outcome though. Devin is now free to go where he chooses; he can even return to San Antonio. But at least for now, he has chosen to stay on with me working as a ranch hand. I gave him the job, but made it conditional. I required that he enroll in courses at Sul Ross State University in Alpine next semester and work towards obtaining a degree."

"That's great news, Mr. Ward," Thibodaux said. "Sometimes things just work out well if you're willing to be patient."

Trenton Ward, his facial expression reflecting satisfaction, stared out his office window for a moment, then looked back at the two men seated across from him.

"You know, when I talked to Devin about his future, we were sitting on the porch of the ranch house. I had never told him about my conversations with Trey when we were at the ranch.

"He said, *Mr. Ward, when I sit out here at night, I can almost sense the presence of the ghosts of Apache Indians and of the Buffalo Soldiers who were stationed down at Fort Davis and lost their lives out here making this place safe for us.* He couldn't have known what it meant to me to hear those words. It was as close to having Trey back as I'll ever get."

Tanner and Thibodaux excused themselves, leaving Trenton Ward to enjoy the reflections about his son. As they drove past the old Fort, now a museum, Thibodaux spoke.

"I was glad to hear Devin knew about the Buffalo Soldiers. They are a part of African-American heritage that young men, black and white, can be proud of. There are far too few such examples in society today. Their ghosts are a part of this area just as much as the Apaches."

Tanner's eyes never left the road as he responded, "I think we've added a couple of less romantic spirits to the mix. I'm not sure those two will evoke such idealistic memories."

Larry Watts resides with his wife and fellow author, Carolyn Ferrell Watts, on the Texas Gulf Coast where both spend time writing, enjoying the Gulf breeze, and practicing HAPPY!

A personal message from Larry:

I hope you enjoyed Rich Man, Dead Man and that you will continue to read my novels. The third in the Tanner & Thibodaux series will be released soon. Please e-mail me at Larry@LarryWatts.net to ask a question or leave a comment. You can visit my website, www.LarryWatts.net to learn more about my novels and other writing.

Also available from Larry Watts

Homicide in Black & White (The Tanner & Thibodaux Crime Series, Book 1) (2014)

The Park Place Rangers, A book of short stories (2014)

Cheating Justice (2013)

Right, Wrong, & Rationalizing Truth (2011)